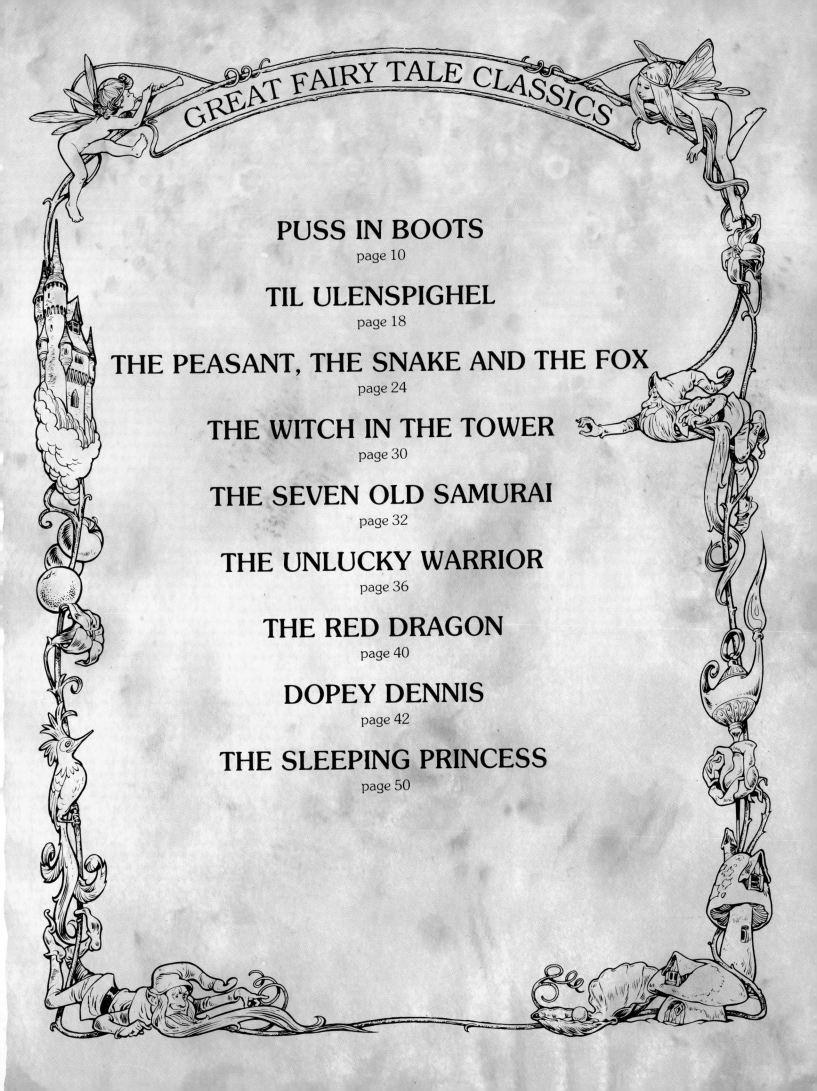

GREAT FAIRY TALE CLASSICS

ILLUSTRATED BY TONY WOLF
TEXT BY PETER HOLEINONE

© DAMI EDITORE, ITALY

Published by Tormont Publications Inc.
338 Saint Antoine St. E.
Montreal, Quebec
CANADA H2Y IA3

Printed in Italy

Printed by Officine Grafiche De Agostini S.p.A.
Bound by Legatoria del Verbano S.p.A.

The story of
PUSS IN BOOTS
and other tales

Once upon a time . . .

a miller died leaving the mill to his eldest son, his donkey to his second son and . . . a cat to his youngest son.

"Now that's some difference!" you might say; but there you are, that's how the miller was!

PUSS IN BOOTS

The eldest son kept the mill, the second son took the donkey and set off in search of his fortune . . . while the third sat down on a stone and sighed,

"A cat! What am I going to do with that?" But the cat heard his words and said,

"Don't worry, Master. What do you think?

That I'm worth less than a half-ruined mill or a mangy donkey? Give me a cloak, a hat with a feather in it, a bag and a pair of boots, and you will see what I can do." The young man, by no means surprised, for it was quite common for cats to talk in those days, gave the cat what he asked for, and as he strode away, confident and cheerful, the cat said, "Don't look so glum, Master. See you soon!"

Swift of foot as he was, the cat caught a fat wild rabbit, popped it into his bag, knocked at the castle gate, went before the King and, removing his hat, with a sweeping bow, he said:

"Sire, the famous Marquis of Carabas sends you this fine plump rabbit as a gift."

"Oh," said the King, "thanks so much."

"Till tomorrow," replied the cat as he went out. And the next day, back he came with some partridges tucked away in his bag. "Another gift from the brave Marquis of Carabas," he

announced. The Queen remarked,

"This Marquis of Carabas is indeed a very courteous gentleman."

In the days that followed, Puss in Boots regularly visited the castle, carrying rabbits, hares, partridges and skylarks, presenting them all to the King in the name of the Marquis of Carabas. Folk at the palace began to talk about this noble gentleman.

"He must be a great hunter," someone remarked. "He must be very loyal to the King," said someone else. And yet another, "But who is he? I've never heard of him." At this someone who wanted to show people how much he knew, replied,

"Oh, yes, I've heard his name before. In fact, I knew his father."

The Queen was very interested in this generous man who sent these gifts. "Is your master young and handsome?" she asked the cat.

"Oh yes. And very rich, too," answered Puss in Boots. "In fact, he would be very honoured if you and the King called to see him in his castle." When the cat returned home and told his master that the King and Queen were going to visit him, he was horrified.

"Whatever shall we do?" he cried. "As soon as they see me they will know how poor I am."

"Leave everything to me," replied Puss in Boots. "I have a plan." For several days, the crafty cat kept on taking gifts to the King and Queen, and one day he discovered that they were taking the Princess on a carriage ride that very afternoon.

The cat hurried home in great excitement. "Master, come along," he cried. "It is time to carry out my plan. You must go for a swim in the river."

"But I can't swim," replied the young man.

"That's all right," replied Puss in Boots. "Just trust me." So they went to the river and when the King's carriage appeared the cat pushed his master into the water.

"Help!" cried the cat. "The Marquis of Carabas is drowning." The King heard his cries and sent his escorts to the rescue. They arrived just in time to save the poor man, who really was drowning. The King, the Queen and the Princess fussed around and ordered new clothes to be brought for the Marquis of Carabas.

"Wouldn't you like to marry such a handsome man?" the Queen asked her daughter.

"Oh, yes," replied the Princess. However, the cat overheard one of the ministers remark that they must find out how rich he was.

"He is very rich indeed," said Puss in Boots. "He owns the castle and all this land. Come and see for yourself. I will meet you at the castle."

And with these words, the cat rushed off in the direction of the castle, shouting at the peasants working in the fields, "If anyone asks you who your master is, answer: the Marquis of Carabas.

Otherwise you will all be sorry." And so, when the King's carriage swept past, the peasants told the King that their master was the Marquis of Carabas.

In the meantime, Puss in Boots had arrived at the castle, the home of a huge, cruel ogre. Before knocking at the gate, the cat said to himself, "I must be very careful, or I'll never get out

of here alive." When the door opened, Puss in Boots removed his feather hat, exclaiming, "My Lord Ogre, my respects!"

"What do you want, cat?" asked the ogre rudely.

"Sire, I've heard you possess great powers. That, for instance, you can change into a lion or an elephant."

"That's perfectly true," said the ogre, "and so what?"

"Well," said the cat, "I was talking to certain friends of mine who said that you can't turn into a tiny little creature, like a mouse."

"Oh, so that's what they say, is it?" exclaimed the ogre. The cat nodded,

"Well, Sire, that's my opinion too, because folk that can do big things never can manage little ones."

"Oh, yes? Well, just watch this!" retorted the ogre, turning into a mouse. In a flash, the cat leapt on the mouse and ate it whole. Then he dashed to the castle gate, just in time, for the King's carriage was drawing up. With a bow, Puss in Boots said,

"Sire, welcome to the castle of the Marquis of Carabas!" The King and Queen, the Princess and the miller's son who, dressed in his princely clothes, really did look like a marquis, got out of the carriage and the King spoke:

"My dear Marquis, you're a fine, handsome, young man, you have a great deal of land and a magnificent castle. Tell me, are you married?"

"No," the young man answered, "but I would like to find a wife." He looked at the Princess as he spoke. She in turn smiled at him.

To cut a long story short, the miller's son, now Marquis of Carabas, married the Princess and lived happily with her in the castle. And from time to time, the cat would wink and whisper, "You see, Master, I am worth a lot more than any mangy donkey or half-ruined mill, aren't I?"

TIL ULENSPIGHEL

Once upon a time there lived a little boy called Til Ulenspighel. His father was a good blacksmith, his mother a kindly woman, but they never imagined that they had brought into the world the naughtiest rascal ever heard of! Til had such a lively personality, bright and naughty, that people couldn't help smiling when they saw him. And he got up to such mischief and all sorts of tricks, that we can't help smiling to ourselves . . . But as you'll soon see, the ones who didn't see the funny side of things were his fellow citizens. The minute he learned to speak, Til pulled people's legs. If a man, for instance, had flat feet, Til would greet him by saying,

"Good day, Mr. Flatfeet!" And if a lady had a red nose, he would say, "Good evening, Mrs. Rednose!" He enjoyed playing tricks and teasing everyone. Of course, the neighbours complained to his father, saying,

"Mr. Ulenspighel, what a rude son you have!" And so, one day, Til's father said to him,

"Listen, son, why don't people like you? Do you annoy them?"

"Who, me?" said Til with an innocent air. "I never bother anyone. It's other people that shake their fists at me whenever they see me and say nasty things."

"Hmm!" said his father. "I wonder if that's really so. I'm going to market with the donkey. Get up behind!" Till didn't need to be told twice and he clambered behind his father.

But the second he was on the donkey's back, he hung a notice on his shoulders on which he had written: 'Whoever reads this is a donkey.' People *did* read it and they were offended, so they shook their fists and shouted, "Oh, you horrid boy, Til! What a little horror you are!" On hearing these shouts, Til's father, who knew nothing about the notice, muttered:

"You're right, Til. People are angry with you, though goodness knows why! Don't worry," he added, "come and sit in front and we'll see if they still call you names." Til did as he was told and slung the notice over his chest. Though his father couldn't see it, he could see other people as they shook their fists, scowled, shouted and yelled insults, and he said, "Folk don't like you, Til. But pay no attention to them and go your own way!" And Til laughed up his sleeve. . . .

Time went by and Til began to weary of long faces every
time people saw him. He joked and teased folk now and again,
but what harm was there in that? All he wanted to do was
amuse himself and others as well. One day, a company of
wandering entertainers came to the town: actors, sword
swallowers and acrobats. They made a great impression on the
lad, who stared at them open-mouthed. While holding a pole in
their hands, they kept their balance as they walked the
tightrope across the road. How he would love to do the same.
The people who now shook their fists at him would clap their
hands. No sooner thought than done, the boy picked up a pole,
stretched a rope between two trees in the wood and started to
practise. Of course, it wasn't easy and he fell more than once.
But in the end, he felt pretty secure and decided to hold a
show. He went through the streets crying,

"Tomorrow, Til Ulenspighel, the acrobat, will walk the
tightrope!" Filled with curiosity, everyone came to watch.

Til had stretched the rope between his balcony and a tree in
the nearby wood: the rope lay above the river and the young

lad climbed on. The crowd that, at first had laughed and made a noise, grew quiet after a while, and were impressed:

"He's clever all right," someone said. "He's a real acrobat," said someone else. "We were wrong about him!"

At that moment, Til's mother, who knew nothing about her son's gymnastics, hearing the murmur of the crowd, went onto the balcony . . . and saw her son walking the rope suspended over empty space. Frightened, she shouted,

"Til, come down at once!" And seeing that the boy was not doing as he was told, she picked up the scissors and cut the rope. Til fell with a splash into the river. You can imagine the people! First they started to laugh, snigger and make fun of the poor lad as he struggled soaking from the water.

"Hey, acrobat! If that had been the ground instead of water, you'd have had a cracked head, wouldn't you?" they called, chuckling, and Til said to himself, "Laugh if you want to, he who laughs last laughs longest! . . ."

Some days later, Til announced he was going to repeat the show, this time not over the river but above the main road. Everyone rushed to watch, hoping to see him fall off and hurt himself. Before he ventured on to the rope, Til called out, "To make it more difficult for me, I'm going to carry a sack on my back. Every spectator will give me his left shoe. I'll put it in the sack and hand it back at the end of the show." Everyone did this. Til walked the tightrope until he reached the middle of the road, and from the heights he said, "Now I'm going to give you back your shoes. There they are!" and opening the sack, he emptied out the shoes.

You can picture the confusion that reigned then. Not only did the onlookers get hit on the head by shoes, but everyone hunted for his own shoe without managing to find it; he'd pick one up, but it belonged to somebody else, and he'd throw it down again, and start to look for another, argue, exchange insults . . . and Til, from a window on high looked down on the pandemonium and chuckling said,

"Ha! He who laughs last laughs longest! . . ."

THE PEASANT, THE SNAKE AND THE FOX

Once upon a time, a peasant on his way home heard a feeble voice calling "Help! Help!" He looked round, took a careful step or two then realised that the sound was coming from beneath a large boulder. He asked in amazement: "Who's that calling?" And a voice replied,

"It's me. The rock rolled down over my hole and I'm shut in. I can't get out, I'm going to die. Please help me. Move the boulder." The peasant then asked:

"But who are you?"

"I'm a poor snake," came the reply.

"A snake? But if I let you out you will bite me."

"No, no, I promise I won't. Get me out, please!" The peasant allowed himself to be persuaded and he shifted the boulder . . . and out of a hole in the ground slid a snake which darted towards the peasant and tried to bite him. The man jumped back and cried,

"Why did you do that?" The snake replied, "Because every good deed is rewarded by an evil one, didn't you know that?"

"No, I didn't. I don't think that's so," said the peasant.

"Very well," said the snake. "Let's go and ask someone. If we come across someone who thinks as you do, well, that's it, but if people say I'm right, then I shall bite you. Agreed?"

"Agreed," said the peasant, and off they went.

A little later, they met an old mangy lame horse, thin and covered in scratches, with an uncombed mane and dirty tail. The peasant spoke to him.

"Listen, friend. If someone does a good deed, what does he get as his reward?" Without a moment's hesitation, the horse replied.

"A bad deed. Look at me! I served my master faithfully for years and now that I'm old, he has left me to die of starvation!" At these words, the snake turned to the peasant and hissed, "Did you hear that? I shall bite you now!" But the man exclaimed: "Wait! One question isn't enough! We have to ask someone else."

"Bother!" exclaimed the snake. "Very well, let's look for someone else, but wait and see, I'm right and I'll get my bite!" So, leaving the horse behind, the pair went on their way.

They met a sheep which, at the peasant's question, said: "A good deed is always repaid with a bad deed. Look at me, I always follow my master and never complain. I obey him all the time and what does he do? He shears my fleece in winter, so I feel the cold, and makes me keep it in summer, so I melt with the heat!"

"Get ready," said the snake, "I'm about to bite!" But the peasant said,

"Please! We've had the first round, and the second one as well, now let's play the deciding round. If I'm wrong at the third question, then I'll let you bite me."

On they went, and in the wood, the peasant caught sight of a fox. Suddenly he had an idea. With an excuse, he left the snake on the road and ran into the wood to speak to the fox.

"Listen, fox, do you too think that a good deed is always rewarded by a bad one?"

"Of course!" replied the fox. Then the man went on.

"Well, listen, I'm going to ask you the same question in front of a snake. If you say that one good deed is rewarded by another good deed, I'll give you a present of a piglet, a lamb or a goose. How's that?"

"Good," said the fox. The peasant went back to the snake.

"I saw a fox over there," he said. "As you know, foxes are wise. Let's go and hear what he thinks about it." A little later they asked the fox the same question and the fox replied as had been agreed.

"A good deed is always rewarded with another good deed, but," he went on, "why ask me that question?"

"Because this snake, that I helped to escape from his hole blocked by a boulder, wants to bite me," replied the peasant. The fox looked at the snake and said, "Hmm! I think a snake can manage to slither under a boulder."

"But it was a big boulder," the snake protested, "and it was blocking the entrance to my den."

"I don't believe you!"

"Oh, don't you? Well come and see then," said the snake, setting off for his den with the fox and the peasant. Pointing to the boulder, he said, "See? That boulder fell just there," and he pointed to the entrance.

But the fox shook his head. "A big snake like you couldn't get into such a little hole," he said. Annoyed, the snake retorted,

"Don't you think so?" and slid swiftly into the hole. Then the fox shouted,

"Quick, peasant man! Shut him in!" and the peasant rolled the boulder back across the mouth of the den, imprisoning the snake (and I think he's in there yet!).

"Ah, fox," said the peasant happily, "now that was a good deed! You got rid of that wicked snake for me! Thanks a million!"

"Oh, it was nothing," replied the fox, "but don't forget that piglet, the lamb and the goose you promised me."

"No, I won't. Come to the farm this evening and you shall have them," said the man.

That same evening, the fox went to the farm, but the peasant appeared with two snarling dogs and a gun, shouting, "Get out of here, you horrible beast, if you don't want to get into trouble!"

The fox trotted away, sad and disappointed, muttering, "and they say I'm cunning! The cunning one is that peasant. Oh, well, that poor snake was probably right, good deeds are repaid with bad deeds," and off he went, his tail between his legs, into the wood.

THE WITCH IN THE TOWER

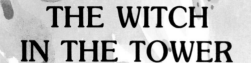

Once upon a time . . . people in the Japanese city of Kyoto were terribly afraid; they shook with fear. A fierce witch had taken possession of the tower over the city gate which she opened and closed whenever she felt like it. She was capable of locking the gate in the face of travellers bringing food and merchandise, or throwing it wide open to savage tribes from the north. Many brave Samurai, the strongest and best fighters, had faced up to the witch, but the minute she set eyes on them, she hurled herself out of the tower, hair flying in the wind, screeching furiously and brandishing a fiery sword. Attacking them one by one, she left them lying dead in the dust. No, there was no hope for the city of Kyoto, and many people began to think of leaving it. The folk were murmuring,

"All our Samurai are dead. If only Watanabi were still here, the bravest of them all! But all that remains is his sword, and there's no one able to use it."

However, the sword was not all that remained of valiant Watanabi, there was also his son, a young boy. On hearing what the citizens were saying, he wondered,

"My father has gone, he died fighting, but we still have his sword. I shall take it and face the witch. Win or die, I shall be a credit to my father's memory." So the boy bravely armed himself and went off to the tower. The witch saw him arrive and she grinned, but did not make a move. She wouldn't even bother using her fiery sword on that snivelling youngster, she would wither him with a glance. So she paid little heed to Watanabi's son as he quietly crept into the tower, climbed the stairs without making the slightest sound and entered the witch's room. When, however, the witch heard the door close, she turned round and laid her wild burning gaze on the boy . . . but the splendour of Watanabi's sword blinded her.

"This is Watanabi's sword!" shouted the young boy, and before the witch could defend herself, he struck a blow and ended her life. In his father's memory and in honour of his sword, the boy had freed the city of Kyoto.

THE SEVEN OLD SAMURAI

Once upon a time, in far off Japan, a band of fierce robbers had their hiding place on top of a mountain almost always covered with grey clouds, windswept and battered by storms. The robbers lived in a large cave where they had piled their spoils. Now and again, they went down the mountain, attacked a village, murdered the poor folk they chanced upon, stole whatever they could lay hands on and burned it to the ground. Wherever the robbers passed, there was nothing but smoking ruins, weeping men and women, misery, mourning and desolation.

The Emperor, worried at this, had sent his soldiers to attack the mountain, but the robbers had always managed to drive them off. The Emperor sent for one of the last remaining Samurai, old Raiko, and said to him:

"Raiko, you've served me for many years. Do my bidding for one last time. Go to the mountain at the head of an army and wipe out these bloodthirsty bandits." Raiko sighed.

"Your Majesty, if I were young again I'd do it alone. Today I'm too old, far too old to do that, or to command an army."

"Must I then," said the Emperor, "submit to the force of these marauding robbers?" The old Samurai replied:

"No, I'll go up there with six Samurai like myself."

"But if they're all as old as you, how can they help you?"

"Have faith in us!" said Raiko.

A few days later, the seven Samurai set off on their journey, not with horses, swords, shields and armour, which they could no longer have worn anyway, but dressed as humble pilgrims. From the summit, the bandits watched them come, and their leader said,

"Who cares about seven beggars. Let them climb up." The seven reached the cave and Raiko humbly said,

"Let us come in, it's cold outside. There's a wind blowing and we, as you can see, are old men. We'll be no trouble to you." The leader of the gang scornfully replied:

"Come in, old men, and stay in a corner." And so the seven pilgrims huddled in a corner while the bandits ate their meal of food stolen from the villages nearby.

Now and again, they threw scraps of food and leftovers to the old men, saying: "Eat this, and it is much too good for you." A few hours later, Raiko rose to his feet saying:

"The wind has dropped. We can go on our way. In thanks for your hospitality, we would like to offer you this liqueur, it is saké, rice wine. Drink our health with it." The robbers needed no second telling. In the blink of an eye, they had emptied the goatskin bottle Raika held out to them. And in the blink of an eye they all lay dead, for the saké contained a very potent poison. And so, the seven Samurai, too old to wield a sword, served the Emperor for the last time.

THE UNLUCKY WARRIOR

Once upon a time there was a Samurai called Hido. Valiant and strong, he was afraid of no-one, yet in all the wars he had ever fought, he had always found himself on the losing side. People in his home town began to say "Hido brings bad luck." And because nobody wanted him to fight for them any more the Samurai ended up a poor man. He said to himself:

"I'll go to a town where no-one knows me. Maybe I'll find work there." He gathered up his remaining belongings, his sword, bow and three arrows, and set off along the first road he came to. On and on he walked, until after many days march, he reached the banks of a lake. As he started to cross the narrow bridge over the water, he stopped in surprise. The way was blocked by an enormous snake, fast asleep. From its mouth and nostrils, it breathed red smoke with a pungent smell of sulphur. Hido thought to himself,

"That beast isn't going to stop *me*," and on tiptoe he stepped over the snake, without wakening it up, and went on his way. But he had barely gone twenty metres when he heard a voice behind him.

"Hey, you! Samurai!" He turned round. The snake had disappeared and in its place stood a well-dressed man, who made a friendly gesture and said,

"You're a brave one! You weren't scared of the snake. You see, I'm looking for a Samurai, and so, whenever I see someone coming, I turn into a snake. So far, you're the only person that has had the courage to step over it. What's your name?"

"Hido," replied the Samurai, "and who are *you*?" The man pointed to the lake.

"I'm King of that realm."

"What!" exclaimed Hido. "Is your realm a lake?" The King replied smiling,

"Yes. But under the water lies a great city protected by a crystal ball. My people live there happily, or at least they were happy until the Dragon arrived."

"The Dragon?" asked Hido. And the King replied sadly,

"Yes. Every second night, he dives off the bridge into the water, enters the crystal ball and creates havoc amongst my subjects. It won't be long before he eats us all. That's why I'm looking for a Samurai!"

Hido understood what he meant. "Do you want me to fight the Dragon?" he asked.

"Yes!"

"I think you ought to know, Sire, that people say I bring bad luck." To which the King replied:

"I never believe what I hear, only what I see. Come with me." He took Hido's hand and they went down into the lake. Wonder of wonders! The waters opened up and they went down to the great crystal circle that contained the city. There, Hido sat down with the King who gave him food and drink. Then he said, "In a little while you will hear a terrible noise. It will be the Dragon. You will have to face him up there, Hido."

"I'm not afraid. I have my sword, bow and three arrows."

"Only *three*? You will need a hundred arrows!" exclaimed the King. But Hido shook his head.

"They're poisoned, but even if they weren't, they would still be enough, because if the Dragon doesn't stop with three arrows in him, I wouldn't have time to fire any more." Just then there was a fearful noise and the sound of shouting.

"The Dragon! The Dragon!" Hido picked up his weapons and ran onto the bridge, only just in time. For the Dragon, huge and terrible, was advancing, with a roar, and breathing fire. Hido fired his first and second arrows, both of them hit the Dragon right in the heart, but it didn't stop.

Just as the Dragon was bearing down ferociously on him, Hido rememberd hearing that the only poison to stop a dragon is a man's saliva. So he licked his fingers and wet the tip of his last arrow, fired and hit the Dragon . . . On it came, still roaring. "All is lost," said Hido to himself . . .

. . . but after taking another step or two, the Dragon stopped in its tracks, shuddered and fell to the ground. It was dead. All the citizens rushed from the lake to greet Hido and shower him with gifts, telling him:

"Oh, brave Samurai, luck is with you and with our people!" So Hido knew that not only had he defeated the Dragon, he had overcome his bad luck.

THE RED DRAGON

Once there was a time, thousands of years ago, when animals were not the same as they are now. Except for a few like the lion, the tiger and the butterflies, they all looked alike. All were more or less the same height, everyone had four legs and it wasn't easy to tell which was which, even though the elephant did weigh more than the hyena, and the hippo more than the gazelle. One day, while all the animals were relaxing in a field, along came a red dragon, out of breath, crying,

"We're in danger, folks! The world is about to come to an end!"

"How do you know?" everyone asked. The dragon replied,

"I read it in the stars. We must escape!"

"But where can we go?" they asked him.

"To another world," he replied. "I'll take you there. I can fly and I'll take you to a planet that is safer than this one." Frightened, as they were, all the animals climbed on to the dragon's back.

With a bored look, the lion said, "I'm not scared of anything, so I'll just stay here on Earth." The others, however, were fighting to get on the dragon's back.

"Don't push, you behind!" shouted the crocodile.

"Hey, move that paw!" It was just like people today pushing and shoving to get onto an overcrowded train. At last the dragon cried,

"Ready! Off we go," and started to run for takeoff. The first and the second runs weren't fast enough, but at the third try he finally got off the ground, flapping his wings and waving his tail.

"Not so fast!" shouted somebody, and another voice yelled: "Faster, or we will end up in the trees!" The dragon replied,

"Oh, bother! I'm doing the best I can. Why don't you lot keep still, for once." The fact was that because they were frightened, they did everything but keep still, and so, after a while, the poor red dragon, now very tired, simply could not flap his wings any longer . . . and crashed on a lovely green meadow.

All the animals shrieked with terror. Nobody lost his life . . . but the snake lost his legs and slithered away through the grass. The rhino bumped his head and grew a horn. All the elephant's teeth fell out, except for two which became very long. The giraffe sprained his neck and it grew to a great length. The hippo rolled about so much he became nearly round, ended up in a pond and didn't come out, he was too ashamed to be seen . . . Well, in that fall, all the animals took on a different appearance and became what they are today. And when the lion saw them, what he said was:

"Oh, how funny you look!"

DOPEY DENNIS

Once upon a time, there was a little boy called Dennis. Everyone called him Dopey because . . . well, read on and you will see why. Dennis lived with his mother in a nice house with a courtyard, vegetable plot, cellar and a henrun. One day his mother, since she had to go shopping, said to him,

"I'll be away for an hour or two, son. Now, the broody hen is sitting on her eggs. Make sure nobody goes near her. Keep the house tidy and don't touch the jar in the cupboard, it's full of poison."

"Don't worry, Mum," the little boy said, and when his mother had gone, he went into the yard to keep guard over the broody hen. However, tired of sitting, the hen got up to stretch her legs for a little before going back to the eggs. Dennis picked up a stick and yelled:

"You nasty creature, get right back on those eggs!"

But the broody hen, annoyed, only said, "Cluck!", and so
Dennis hit her with his stick. He didn't really mean to do her
any harm, but the blow fell on the middle of her neck and the
poor hen dropped dead.

"Oh!" gasped the lad. "Who's going to sit on the eggs now?
Well, I had better do something about that!" So he sat on the
eggs . . . and broke the lot! Getting up with the seat of his
trousers sticky with egg yolk, Dennis said to himself, "Mum will
give me such a scolding. But to keep in her good books, I'll
give her a surprise, I'll make the lunch." He picked up the hen,
plucked its feathers and put it on the spit to roast.

"A roast calls for a good wine!" he said to himself. He took a
jug and went down to the cellar where he started to draw
sparkling red wine from a barrel. "Mum will be pleased with
me," he told himself. At that moment, there was a dreadful
noise in the kitchen. Dennis said to himself, "Who can that be? I
must go and see." And he went . . . forgetting to turn off the tap
on the barrel.

Up he ran to the kitchen and saw the cat with the roast hen in its jaws and the spit overturned. "Hey thief!" shouted the lad. "Put my hen down!" He picked up a rolling pin and started to chase the cat which, terrified as it was, firmly held on to the roast chicken as it dashed from room to room. The pair of them knocked against the cupboards, overturned tables, sideboards and stools, smashed vases, pots, plates and glasses. The devastation ended when the cat dropped the hen, leapt out of a window and vanished from sight. Dennis picked up his roast, laid it on the table and said:

"Now, I'll go and fetch the wine." He went back to the cellar . . . which was flooded with the wine that had poured out of the barrel. "Good gracious!" gasped Dennis. "What am I to do now?" He didn't dare go in, for before him streched a lake of red wine.

"I'll have to mop it all up," muttered Dennis to himself, "but how? I could go into the yard and get some sacks of sand, bring them into the cellar and scatter the sand over the floor . . . But that's much too hard work. I'd better think of something else, now then . . ." Seated on the bottom step, his elbows on his knees, holding his head in his hands, the lad tried to think of a good idea. It really was an alarming situation: there were nearly six inches of wine all over the floor and in it floated corks, bottles and bits of wood . . .

"I've got it!" Dennis suddenly exclaimed. He picked up one of the bags lying on a table, opened it . . . and started to scatter all the flour it contained. "Splendid! The flour will absorb the wine and I can walk about the cellar without wetting my feet," he cried.

In no time at all, he had spread not one but five bags of good flour on the floor. In the end, the floor was covered with a wine-coloured, soft, sticky paste, and as he walked on it, it stuck to his shoes. Dennis went to get the jug he had filled and carried it in great delight back to the table, leaving red footprints everywhere.

"Mum is going to be really pleased," he said.

Nevertheless, when he thought of all the mess he had made, he began to fear a scolding and maybe punishment too. "Never mind," he said, "I'll drink the poison and die." So he went to the cupboard and picked up the jar. He thought the poison would be a black liquid, but the jar contained a red cream. He picked up a spoon and said, "I'll eat it then instead of drinking it."

Just as he was about to take his first spoonful, he realised how silly he was. Nobody should ever eat poison, not even when your name is Dopey Dennis. Instead, he decided to hide from his mother so that she would not be able to punish him.

A quarter of an hour later, his mother returned. When she saw the overturned furniture, the broken plates and the red footprints, she got a fright and cried, "Dennis! What has happened? Where are you? Answer me!"

There was no reply, but she suddenly noticed a pair of legs sticking out of the oven.

"I'm not surprised you are hiding from me, Dennis, after causing all this mess," she said. "Well, while I am clearing up after you, you can take this roll of cloth to the market and try and sell it for a good price." And she handed the boy a roll of cloth as she spoke. "Oh, I will," said Dennis. "Leave it to me."

When he got to market, Dennis began to shout, "Cloth! Who'll buy this lovely cloth?" Several women came over and asked him,

"What kind of cloth is it? Is it soft? Is it hard-wearing? Is it dear? How long is it? How much does it cost"? Dennis exclaimed:

"You talk too much, and I don't sell things to chatterboxes," and off he went. He passed by a statue and mistook it for a fine gentleman, so he asked it, "Sir, would you like to buy this fine cloth? Yes or no? If you don't say anything, that means you do. Look here! Do you like it? Yes? Good! Then take it," and he left the cloth beside the statue and went home.

"Mum! Mum!" he cried. "I've sold the cloth to a very well-dressed gentleman!" The woman asked:

"How much did he give you for it?" Dennis muttered,

"Oh! I forgot to ask him for the money! Don't worry, I'll go and ask him for it." He ran back to the statue but the cloth had gone. Someone had clearly taken it away. Said Dennis to the statue, "I see you've taken the cloth home already. Fine, now give me the money!" Of course, the statue did not reply. Dennis repeated his request, then losing his temper, he picked up a stick and began to beat the statue about the head . . . which broke off and rolled to the ground. Out of the head poured a handful of gold coins, hidden there by goodness knows who! Dennis picked up the coins, put the head back in position and went home.

"Look!" he called. And his mother stared in astonishment at this small fortune.

"Who gave you such a good price?" his mother asked him. The lad replied:

"A very dignified-looking gentleman. He didn't speak, and do you know where he kept his money? In his head!" At this, Dennis's mother exclaimed:

"Dennis, listen! You killed the broody hen, broke the eggs, flooded the cellar with wine, wasted five bags of flour, smashed plates, bottles, vases and glasses; you nearly ate the cream, if you think you're going to pull my leg as well, you're badly mistaken! Get out of here!" And grabbing the broom, she chased him out of the house.

"I don't want to see you again till tonight. Off you go into the vegetable plot." But, as the boy was sitting on the doorstep and did not budge, his exasperated mother picked up the first thing that came within her grasp and hurled it at Dennis's head. It was a big basket of dried figs and sultanas. Dennis shouted then:

"Mum! Mum! Quick! Bring a bag! It's raining dry figs and sultanas!" His mother slumped into a chair and said sorrowfully:

"What can I do with a boy like him?"

Now, since Dennis went about telling folk he had a lot of gold coins, the magistrates sent for him. "Where did you find those coins?" they asked him. Dennis replied:

"A gentleman gave me them in payment for a roll of cloth."

"What gentleman?" said the magistrates severely.

"The gentleman that is always standing at the corner of Plane Tree Street and Jasmine Road," replied the boy.

"But that's a statue!" gasped the magistrates. Dennis said:

"He didn't say what his name was, but maybe it is Mr. Statue. He kept his money in his head." The magistrates gaped at each other in utter astonishment. Then the chief magistrate asked:

"Tell us, Dennis, when did you do this piece of business?"

"It was the day it rained dry figs and sultanas!" the boy replied. Again the magistrates exchanged looks, and now certain that Dennis really was dopey, they said:

"You can go home, lad, you're free!"

And so Dennis went home and lived there happily with his mother. A bit dopey, yes, but he never did anybody any harm, and that's all that counts.

THE SLEEPING PRINCESS

Once upon a time there was a Queen who had a beautiful baby daughter. She asked all the fairies in the kingdom to the christening, but unfortunately forgot to invite one of them, who was a bit of a witch as well. She came anyway, but as she passed the baby's cradle, she said:

"When you are sixteen, you will injure yourself with a spindle and die!"

"Oh, no!" screamed the Queen in horror. A good fairy quickly chanted a magic spell to change the curse. When she hurt herself, the girl would fall into a very deep sleep instead of dying.

The years went by, the little Princess grew and became the most beautiful girl in the whole kingdom. Her mother was always very careful to keep her away from spindles, but the Princess, on her sixteenth birthday, as she wandered through the castle, came into a room where an old servant was spinning.

"What are you doing?" she asked the servant.

"I'm spinning. Haven't you seen a spindle before?"

"No. Let me see it!" The servant handed the girl the spindle
. . . and she pricked herself with it and, with a sigh, dropped to the floor.

The terrified old woman hurried to tell the Queen. Beside herself with anguish, the Queen did her best to awaken her daughter but in vain. The court doctors and wizards were called, but there was nothing they could do. The girl could not be wakened from her deep sleep. The good fairy who managed to avoid the worst of the curse came too, and the Queen said to her,

"When will my daughter waken?"

"I don't know," the fairy admitted sadly.

"In a year's time, ten years or twenty?" the Queen went on.

"Maybe in a hundred years' time. Who knows?" said the fairy.

"Oh! What would make her waken?" asked the Queen weeping.

"Love," replied the fairy. "If a man of pure heart were to fall in love with her, that would bring her back to life!"

"How can a man fall in love with a sleeping girl?" sobbed the Queen, and so heart-broken was she that, a few days later, she died. The sleeping Princess was taken to her room and laid on the bed surrounded by garlands of flowers. She was so beautiful, with a sweet face, not like those of the dead, but pink like

those who are sleeping peacefully. The good fairy said to herself,

"When she wakens, who is she going to see around her? Strange faces and people she doesn't know? I can never let that happen. It would be too painful for this unfortunate girl."

So the fairy cast a spell; and everyone that lived in the castle – soldiers, ministers, guards, servants, ladies, pages, cooks, maids and knights – all fell into a deep sleep, wherever they were at that very moment.

"Now," thought the fairy, "when the Princess wakes up, they too will awaken, and life will go on from there." And she left the castle, now wrapped in silence. Not a sound was to be heard, nothing moved except for the clocks, but when they too ran down, they stopped, and time stopped with them. Not even the faintest rustle was to be heard, only the wind whistling round the turrets, not a single voice, only the cry of birds.

The years sped past. In the castle grounds, the trees grew tall. The bushes became thick and straggling, the grass invaded the courtyards and the creepers spread up the walls. In a hundred years, a dense forest grew up.

Now, it so happened that a Prince arrived in these parts. He was the son of a king in a country close by. Young, handsome and melancholy, he sought in solitude everything he could not find in the company of other men: serenity, sincerity and purity. Wandering on his trusty steed he arrived, one day, at the dark forest. Being adventurous, he decided to explore it. He made his way through slowly and with a struggle, for the trees and bushes grew in a thick tangle. A few hours later, now losing heart, he was about to turn his horse and go back when he thought he could see something through the trees . . . He pushed back the branches . . . Wonder of wonders! There in front of him stood a castle with high towers. The young man stood stock still in amazement,

"I wonder who this castle belongs to?" he thought.

The young Prince rode on towards the castle. The drawbridge was down and, holding his horse by the reins, he crossed over it. Immediately he saw the inhabitants draped all over the steps, the halls and courtyards, and said to himself,

"Good heavens! They're dead!" But in a moment, he realised that they were sound asleep. "Wake up! Wake up!" he shouted, but nobody moved. Still thoroughly astonished, he went into the castle and again discovered more people, lying fast asleep on the floor. As though led by a hand in the complete silence, the Prince finally reached the room where the beautiful Princess lay fast asleep. For a long time he stood gazing at her face, so full of serenity, so peaceful, lovely and pure, and he felt spring to his heart that love he had always been searching for and never found. Overcome by emotion, he went close, lifted the girl's little white hand and gently kissed it . . .

At that kiss, the Princess quickly opened her eyes, and wakening from her long long sleep, seeing the Prince beside her, murmured:

"Oh, you have come at last! I was waiting for you in my dream. I've waited so long!"

Just then, the spell was broken. The Princess rose to her feet, holding out her hand to the Prince. And the whole castle woke up too. Everybody rose to their feet and they all stared round in amazement, wondering what had happened. When they finally realised, they rushed to the Princess, more beautiful and happier then ever.

A few days later, the castle that only a short time before had lain in silence, now rang with the sound of singing, music and happy laughter at the great party given in honour of the Prince and Princess, who were getting married. They lived happily ever after, as they always do in fairy tales, not quite so often, however, in real life.